W9-BMO-316

Flatfoot Fox

and the Case of the Bashful Beaver

Flatfoot Fox

and the Case of the Bashful Beaver

ETH CLIFFORD

Illustrated by Brian Lies

GO ASK
FLATFOOT
FOX!

DON'T GIVE
UP OR
PACK
IT IN—

Houghton Mifflin Company

Boston 1995

This one is for my little cousin Rachel W.
in New York who is Flatfoot Fox's number one fan
— E. C.

For Robert M. Pope
— B. L.

Library of Congress Cataloging-in-Publication Data

Clifford, Eth, 1915–
   Flatfoot Fox and the case of the Bashful Beaver / by Eth Clifford;
   illustrated by Brian Lies.
      p. cm.
   Summary: Although Flatfoot Fox is fairly certain that he knows who
stole Bashful Beaver's buttons, the smartest detective in the world
allows his assistant, Secretary Bird, to try to solve the case.
   ISBN 0-395-70560-6
   [1. Mystery and detective stories.   2. Foxes—Fiction.
3. Animals—Fiction.]   I. Lies, Brian, ill. II. Title.
PZ7.C62214Fh 1995   94-14761
[E]—dc20   CIP
                 AC

Printed in the United States of America

BP 10 9 8 7 6 5 4 3 2 1

Contents

1.

A Battered Box of
Broken Bottles

Tap! Tap! Tap!

Someone was tapping on the door. It was such a soft sound, Flatfoot Fox and Secretary Bird weren't sure they heard it.

Tap! Tap! Tap!

There it was again.

"Who can that be?" Secretary Bird asked.

Flatfoot Fox was the smartest detective in the whole world. But even he didn't know who it could be.

"I see a shadow on the door," he said. "But I don't know whose shadow it is. Whoever you are," he shouted, "come in."

The door opened slowly. Very, very slowly. A

head appeared. Then the head disappeared.

"How strange," Secretary Bird said.

"Not so strange when you know who it is," Flat-foot Fox explained. He called out, "Don't be afraid. Come in."

This time the door opened all the way. Bashful Beaver tiptoed in. He went and stood in a corner. He looked up. He looked down. He looked every-where except at Flatfoot Fox and Secretary Bird.

"Do you have a problem?" Flatfoot Fox asked.

Bashful Beaver nodded. "Yes," he whispered. "I have a terrible problem."

He stopped talking.

"I am the smartest detective in the whole world," Flatfoot Fox said, after a while. "But there is one thing I can't do. I can't read minds."

Bashful Beaver sighed. Then he swallowed. He swallowed and sighed, and sighed and swallowed.

"Let me guess," said Flatfoot Fox. "Has someone stolen something from you?"

Bashful Beaver nodded.

"And that something was . . ." Flatfoot Fox began.

"My big black bag of beautiful bright blue buttons," Bashful Beaver said quickly.

"Buttons?" Secretary Bird was angry. "You came to the smartest detective in the whole world about *buttons?*"

"Well, they were my very best buttons."

Flatfoot Fox shook his head at Secretary Bird. "You were right to come," he told Bashful Beaver. "I will take your case. But I need to ask some questions first."

"You want to ask questions before or after?" Bashful Beaver asked.

"Before or after what?" Flatfoot Fox was puzzled.

"Before or after I tell you what happened next."

"Tell me now," Flatfoot Fox ordered.

"Yes. You must tell us now," Secretary Bird agreed.

"Whoever took my big black bag of beautiful bright blue buttons left a battered box of broken bottles behind."

"That's ridiculous," said Secretary Bird. "That's the most ridiculous thing I have ever heard. Why would anyone leave a battered box of broken bottles behind?"

"I don't know," Bashful Beaver said. "That's why I need a detective."

"Hmmmm," said Flatfoot Fox. "Hmmmm," he said again. He was thinking very hard.

"Don't talk," Secretary Bird warned Bashful Beaver, who was opening his mouth to speak. "Can't you see he's thinking? Thinking is hard work."

"Do you think?" Bashful Beaver wondered.

"Not if I can help it," Secretary Bird said. "But I like to watch Flatfoot Fox think."

They both watched Flatfoot Fox think.

At last Bashful Beaver couldn't wait any longer.

"Do you know who took my big black bag of beautiful bright blue buttons? Now that you've done so much thinking?" he asked.

Flatfoot Fox nodded. "Yes. I have a good idea who the thief might be."

"You know who the thief is already?" Secretary Bird was disappointed. "But that's not right. First you have to find suspects and ask questions and look for clues. Then you solve the mystery."

"I said I had a good idea who the thief is," Flatfoot Fox explained. "But a good idea isn't enough. I have to prove it. So the mystery is not solved. Not yet," he said, and hurried out the door.

Bashful Beaver and Secretary Bird stared at each other. Then they ran out after Flatfoot Fox.

2.

Slippery Slivers of Soap

"Wait!" Secretary Bird shouted, as they raced to catch up with Flatfoot Fox.

Flatfoot Fox stopped running until the other two caught up with him.

"You are going about this case all wrong," Secretary Bird insisted. "We must do what you always do — find suspects, ask questions, look for clues. That is how you always work. That is how you must work now."

"Why?" Flatfoot Fox wanted to know.

"Because that is what you do when you're a detective," Secretary Bird insisted again.

"But this case is different," Flatfoot Fox tried to explain.

"No! NO! **NO!!!**" Secretary Bird shouted. "If you can't do it right, I will have to take over."

Flatfoot Fox laughed. "You want to be the smartest detective in the whole world? All right. Go ahead. You solve this mystery."

"Can he do it?" Bashful Beaver asked.

"Shhhh!" Secretary Bird whispered. "There's our first suspect now."

He pointed at Scatterbrain Squirrel, who was halfway down a tree. At first he seemed to be coming down. Then he turned and began to go up. Then he stopped.

"What are you doing?" Secretary Bird called.

"I'm going down the tree. No, wait. I think I was going up."

Secretary Bird shook his head. "That one never knows whether he is coming or going. Stop shilly-shallying," he shouted, "and come down at once."

Scatterbrain Squirrel raced down. "Oh, thank you. Now I remember, I came down to get my savory scrunchy scrumptious seeds . . ."

"Never mind all that," Secretary Bird interrupted. "I must ask you some questions. So be very still."

Scatterbrain Squirrel did as he was told. Not even his long, bushy tail moved. He just stared at Secretary Bird with his bright brown eyes.

"Now then." Secretary Bird felt very important. "Tell me. Why did you steal Bashful Beaver's big black bag of beautiful bright blue buttons?"

"Buttons?" Scatterbrain Squirrel asked. "What's a button? Is it tastier than an acorn? Can you plant it?"

18

Flatfoot Fox grinned. "You want to plant a button like an acorn?"

"I'm the detective now," Secretary Bird said, sounding annoyed. "Now then, do you want to plant a button like an acorn? Whatever for?"

"Well, when an acorn is planted, a big oak tree grows. If you plant a button, what do you get? A button tree?"

19

"What a wonderful idea," Bashful Beaver said. A dreamy look came into his eyes. "A button tree. Lots and lots of button trees."

Flatfoot Fox shook his head, but before he could say anything Secretary Bird shouted, "Can we please get on with questioning this suspect? Wait a minute!" he yelled at Scatterbrain Squirrel, who was running away. "Where do you think you're going?"

"I'm going to get my savory scrunchy scrumptious seeds which I stored in a smashing sky-blue shoe." And he vanished from sight.

"Did you see that?" Bashful Beaver was surprised. "One second he was here. The next second he vanished. How did he do that?"

Before anyone could answer, a long, terrible scream sent shivers up and down everyone's spine. Bashful Beaver ran and hid behind a bush. He shook so hard his teeth rattled. Secretary Bird's legs knocked against each other. His feathers stood straight up in the air.

But Flatfoot Fox ran toward the scream. He shouted back at the others, "You can come out now."

Bashful Beaver tore a branch off the bush and tried to hide behind it as he walked slowly toward Flatfoot Fox.

Secretary Bird smoothed down his feathers. He pretended he hadn't been the least bit scared.

21

3.
Thirty Teeny-Tiny Thimbles

"I went to your place and you weren't there," snapped Mean-Tempered Turtle.

"Why is he snapping at you?" Bashful Beaver asked.

"He's a snapping turtle," Flatfoot Fox explained. "It's what snapping turtles do."

"He's not the least bit pleasant," Secretary Bird said.

"You wouldn't be pleasant, either, if someone stole your collection of tangled tags and tattered tassels," said Mean-Tempered Turtle.

"Is that why you were looking for me?" asked Flatfoot Fox. "Because someone stole your collection of tangled tags and tattered tassels? And left behind what?" he went on.

Mean-Tempered Turtle was surprised. "How did you know the thief left something behind?"

"Never mind how he knew," Secretary Bird began, but Bashful Beaver put in quickly, "What did he leave behind?"

"Thirty teeny-tiny thimbles and twenty-two tousled theses and thoses."

"What are theses and thoses?" Bashful Beaver asked.

"Thingumadoodles, of course," Mean-Tempered Turtle said.

"Thingumadoodles? What's a thingumadoodle?" asked Secretary Bird.

"A flumadiddle." Mean-Tempered Turtle looked surprised. "Everybody knows that."

Secretary Bird whispered to Flatfoot Fox, "I hear him talking, but I don't understand a word he's saying."

"Never mind," Mean-Tempered Turtle shouted. "I know who did it, and I want you to get him."

Now Secretary Bird became angry. What was the use of being a detective if someone else solved the case? And how could anyone who spoke of thingumadoodles and flumadiddles solve anything at all?

"How do you know who the thief is?" he yelled at Mean-Tempered Turtle. "What proof do you have?"

"It's Rinse-Away Raccoon," Mean-Tempered Turtle said.

"Why Rinse-Away Raccoon?" Flatfoot Fox wanted to know.

"Yes — why Rinse-Away Raccoon?" Secretary Bird echoed.

"He wears a mask, doesn't he? You know any-
body else who wears a mask?"

"I say we go get him," said Scatterbrain Squirrel.

"All right," Secretary Bird agreed. "But I'll
ask the questions." And off he ran toward the
river.

4.
Really Rubbery Roots

They all followed Secretary Bird quickly, but they had not gone far when they met him on his way back. With him was Rinse-Away Raccoon. As soon as Rinse-Away Raccoon saw Flatfoot Fox, he began to complain.

"You call yourself a detective?" he asked.

"I *am* a detective," said Flatfoot Fox. "The smartest detective in the whole world."

"Then why aren't you at home when someone needs you?" Rinse-Away Raccoon wanted to know.

"Exactly what I asked him," Mean-Tempered Turtle said.

Flatfoot Fox shook his head. "All right. Tell me. What has been stolen from you?"

Rinse-Away Raccoon's jaw dropped. "How did you know something was stolen?"

"Never mind that," Secretary Bird told him. "Just get on with it. What was stolen?"

"What was stolen? I'll tell you what was stolen. Some rascal stole my rather remarkable raspberry, raisin, rice and ripe red radish relish."

"And what did he leave behind?" Flatfoot Fox wanted to know.

"You really are the smartest detective in the whole world!" said Rinse-Away Raccoon. "That same rascal left behind a mess of revolting, rotten, really rubbery roasted roots."

"How disgusting," Bashful Beaver said.

"Dreadful," Scatterbrain Squirrel said.

"Disgraceful," Mean-Tempered Turtle said.

"Detestable," Secretary Bird agreed.

Flatfoot Fox shook his head. "Not really," he told them. "Not when you know who did it, and why." He looked at Secretary Bird and asked, "Do you still want to be the detective in this case?"

Secretary Bird cleared his throat. He didn't seem to want to answer that question. But when he saw how angry the others were, he finally said, "I think it might be a good idea for you to solve this mystery."

"Good," Flatfoot Fox said. "Now we can get on with it. Follow me. But be very, very quiet, all of you."

When Flatfoot Fox moved on, the others followed on tiptoe.

5.
This for That

Soon Flatfoot Fox stopped walking. He said, "Shhhh," very softly. Then he hid behind a bush. He motioned for the others to do the same. Soon they could hear someone talking.

Flatfoot Fox peered out from behind some leaves. The others did the same.

Rat-a-Tat Rat came along the path. He was pushing a small wheelbarrow and talking to himself. As everyone watched, Rat-a-Tat Rat stopped walking to stare down at the ground.

"Well, will you look at this?" he said.

"Who is he talking to?" Secretary Bird whispered.

"He always talks to himself," Flatfoot Fox whispered back. "Shhhh."

"What a beautiful key!" Rat-a-Tat Rat cried. "It's the biggest key I've ever seen." He looked through the things he had on the wheelbarrow. Then he said, "This for that. I'll leave this comb for the key." He put the key in the wheelbarrow and the comb on the path. Then he moved on.

Rat-a-Tat Rat had only gone a little way when he stopped again. "A mirror," he exclaimed. "Just what I've always wanted." He looked through the wheelbarrow again. "Marvelous!" he cried. "Marbles. Marbles for the mirror. This for that. Perfect." He put the marbles on the path.

"What's the matter with him?" Secretary Bird asked.

"Later," Flatfoot Fox said. "I'll explain later."

Rat-a-Tat Rat began to push his wheelbarrow again. As he skipped along the path, he noticed a long, thick, new nail.

"This is the best nail I have ever found," he cried. "It's the only nail I've ever found. I must have it."

36

Once again he searched through his wheelbarrow. "Perfect," he told himself. "I'll leave these noodles for the nail. This for that," he said, as he left
the nail in the wheelbarrow and put the noodles on
the path.

"I've seen enough," said Flatfoot Fox. He came out from behind his bush. The others popped out, too.

Rat-a-Tat Rat leaped back in surprise. Then he said happily, "Have you come to trade?"

"No," Flatfoot Fox told him. "They have come to take back the things you took from them."

"Thief!" Mean-Tempered Turtle shouted. "Give me back my tangled taps and tattered tassels."

"But . . ." Rat-a-Tat Rat said.

"And I want —" Scatterbrain Squirrel began, but Bashful Beaver interrupted him.

"You stole my big black bag of beautiful bright blue buttons," he cried.

"And you took my rather remarkable raspberry, raisin, rice and ripe red radish relish," Rinse-Away Raccoon said angrily.

"I never stole anything in my life," Rat-a-Tat Rat shouted. "I don't steal. I trade. I'm a trader."

Flatfoot Fox shook his head. "It isn't trading unless you get permission to take something."

"Permission? *Permission?* To trade? What a strange idea." Rat-a-Tat Rat turned to the others and asked, "Didn't you like the things I traded with you?"

"NO!" said Bashful Beaver.

"Certainly not!" said Scatterbrain Squirrel.

"Never," said Mean-Tempered Turtle.

"Will you trade back what you took for what you left?" asked Rinse-Away Raccoon.

"Of course," said Rat-a-Tat Rat. "I love to trade."

Flatfoot Fox and Secretary Bird went along to make sure that Rat-a-Tat Rat kept his word.

First they went back to the river, where Rat-a-Tat Rat took back the rubbery roasted roots and returned the ripe red radish relish. When they left, Rinse-Away looked up at the sign he had put on a tree on the riverbank. It said Food Rinsed While You Wait. Rinse-Away Raccoon walked into the water and called back, in a happy voice, "Don't forget to bring your food. I'll rinse it for free!"

Next, Mean-Tempered Turtle was offered his collection of tangled tags and tattered tassels, but he had changed his mind. He wanted to keep the thirty teeny-tiny thimbles and twenty-two tousled theses and thoses. Especially those twenty-two tousled theses and thoses.

But Scatterbrain Squirrel was happy to have his savory scrunchy scrumptious seeds and his smashing sky-blue shoe back again.

And Bashful Beaver was glad to have his big black bag of beautiful bright blue buttons returned.

On the way home, Secretary Bird was very thoughtful. Then he sighed.

"I was so sure this was one case I could solve," he told Flatfoot Fox. "After all, when you think about it, it was an easy mystery to solve."

Flatfoot Fox didn't answer.

He just grinned.

6.
Fantastically Fearless
Flatfoot Fox

All the way home, Secretary Bird was very quiet. Flatfoot Fox looked at him once in a while, then turned away to hide his smile. He knew why Secretary Bird was angry.

When they were home at last, Secretary Bird slammed the door shut. "It isn't fair," he said. "It just isn't fair!"

"What isn't fair?" asked Flatfoot Fox.

"You knew all the time that Rat-a-Tat Rat was the thief, but you didn't tell me."

"You didn't let me," Flatfoot Fox reminded Secretary Bird. "You wanted to find suspects, ask questions, and look for clues, remember?"

"I could have solved this case if I knew what you knew."

Flatfoot Fox laughed. "If you knew what I know, then I wouldn't be the smartest detective in the whole world. You would be."

"I have a wonderful idea," Secretary Bird said. "Why don't you tell me everything you know, right now?"

"Everything?" Flatfoot Fox shook his head. "That would take a very long time."

"I don't mind." Secretary Bird settled back with an eager look in his eyes.

So Flatfoot Fox began to speak. He kept his voice low and soft. Soon Secretary Bird's eyes began to close. Before long, he was fast asleep.

He didn't hear a knock on the door. Flatfoot Fox went on tiptoe to open it. Then he whispered, "Shhh. My assistant is sleeping. He is all worn out from trying to solve our latest case."

"Let him sleep," the visitor said, very quietly. "Are you Flatfoot Fox? The famous fantastically fearless Flatfoot Fox, who solves marvelously mystifying memorable mysteries?"

"I am," said Flatfoot Fox.

"In that case, we need you," the visitor said.

"Of course you do," said Flatfoot Fox. "Every-body does."